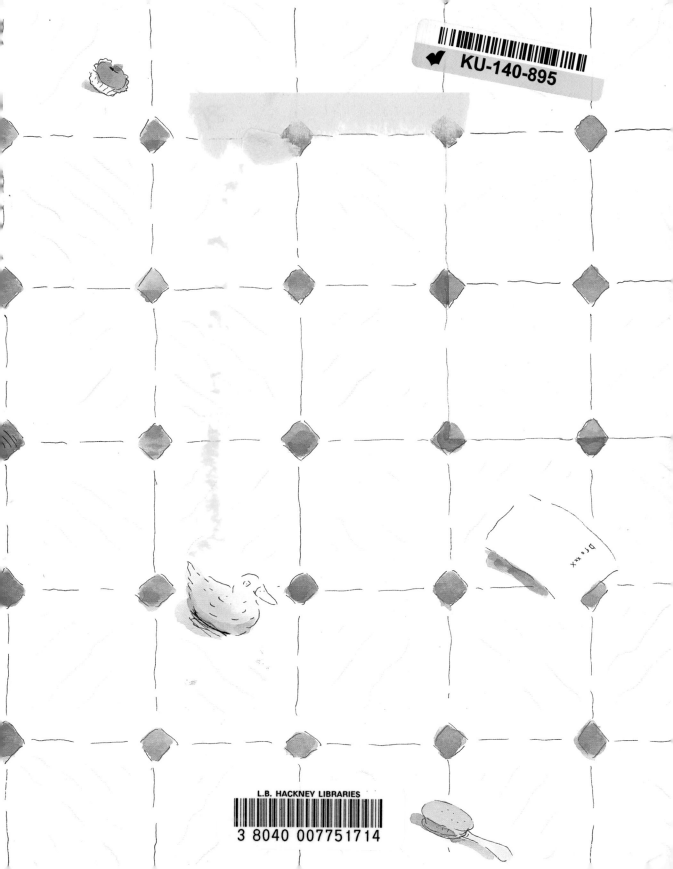

For Chloe and Theo

First published 1986 by
Walker Books Ltd
87 Vauxhall Walk
London SE11 5HJ

This edition published 1996

2 4 6 8 10 9 7 5 3 1

© 1986 Charlotte Voake

Printed in Hong Kong

British Library Cataloguing in Publication Data
A catalogue record for this book is available
from the British Library.

ISBN 0-7445-5508-6

TOM'S CAT

WRITTEN AND ILLUSTRATED BY

Charlotte Voake

WALKER BOOKS

AND SUBSIDIARIES

LONDON • BOSTON • SYDNEY

Here is Tom

looking for his cat.

CLICK CLICK CLICK

Is that Tom's cat

walking across the floor?

No. It's Grandma
knitting socks again.

click click click

TAP TAP TAP

Is that Tom's cat?

Is he dancing on the table?

No.

Tom's mother is typing

a letter to her friend.

tap tap tap

SPLASH SPLASH SPLASH

Is that Tom's cat?

No. Cats hate water.

So does Tom's brother.
But here he is,
trying to wash his hair.

CLATTER

CLATTER

CLATTER

What's that?

Is that Tom's cat bringing everyone a cup of tea?

No.

That's Tom's dad...

making pancakes.

And what's this loud noise?

VROOM

VROOM

VROOM

It sounds a bit like

Tom's cat on a...

MOTORBIKE!

But no.

It's Tom's sister

quickly cleaning the carpet

before anyone sees

she's dropped the cake

on the floor.

So where is Tom's cat?

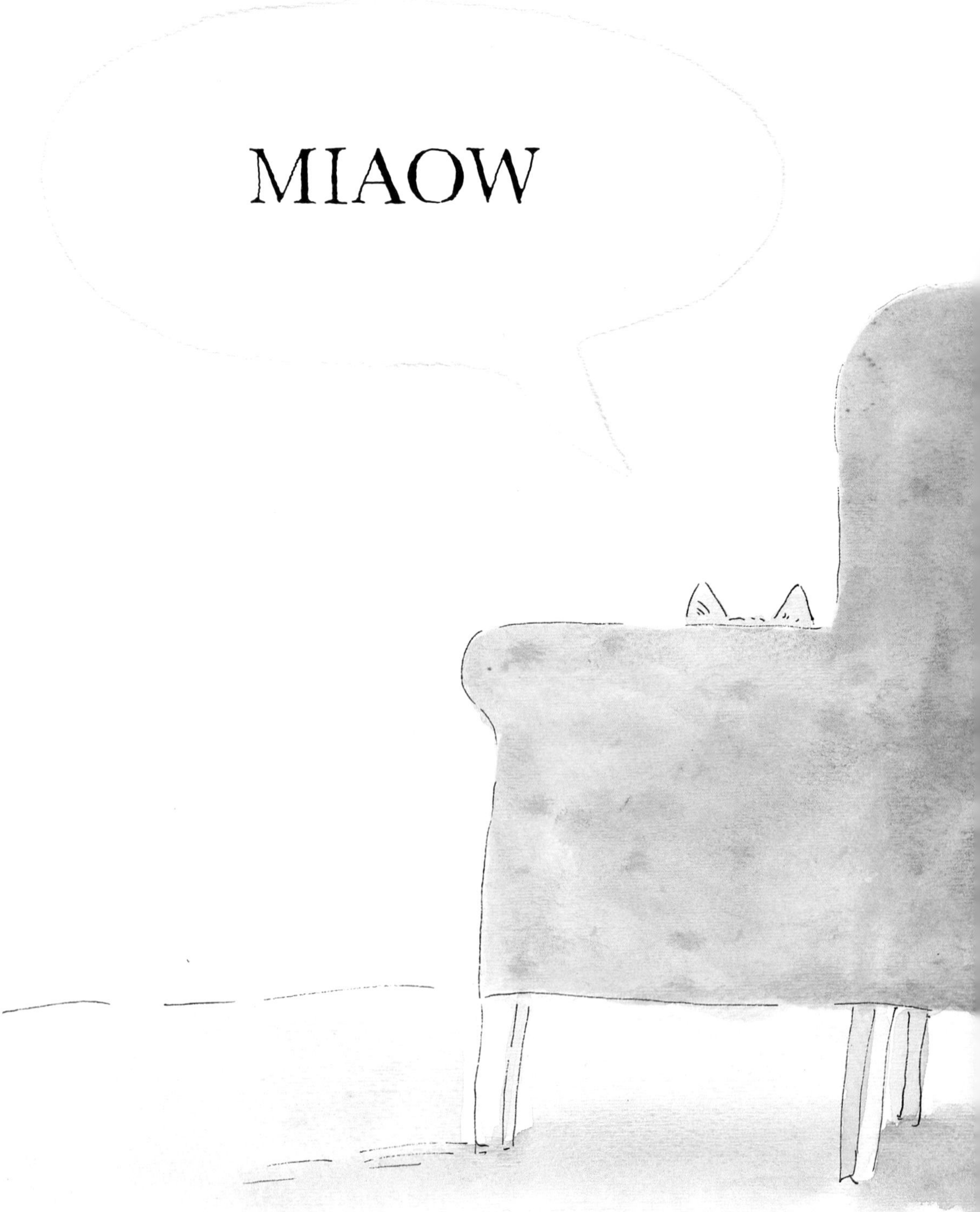
MIAOW